THE THREE WISHES

Pictures by **Yuri Salzman**

Retold by **M. Jean Craig**

SCHOLASTIC INC.

New York   Toronto   London   Auckland   Sydney

W9-BSM-942

ISBN 0-590-41744-4

Copyright © 1968 by M. Jean Craig.
Illustrations copyright © 1986 by Yuri Salzman.
All rights reserved. Published by Scholastic Inc.
Art direction/design by Diana Hrisinko.

12 11 10 9 8 7 6

Printed in the U.S.A.

1/9

24

ONCE UPON A TIME, a long, long time ago, there was a poor wood-cutter. He lived with his wife in a little hut near the great forest.

Every day the wood-cutter went into the forest to work.
He took with him his sharp axe.
And he took a bottle of cold tea and a bag of bread for his lunch.

The wood-cutter worked very hard, every day of the week. But he stayed very poor. And he was tired of being poor. "I never have anything I want," the wood-cutter said. "I wish I had a warm coat. I wish we had a bigger house."

"I wish I had a little cart to carry the wood," the wood-cutter said.
"I wish we could eat roast beef sometimes, and apple pie." But the wood-cutter's wishes did not come true.
One morning when the wood-cutter was looking for wood, he saw a big oak tree. He was very pleased.
"What a lot of wood for me!" he said.
"First I will cut it down. Then I will cut it up!"

He put his bottle of cold tea on the ground.
He put his bag of bread on the ground.
He swung his sharp axe high over his head.
"Oh, don't!" he heard someone say behind him.
The wood-cutter turned and saw...a tree fairy!

The wood-cutter had never seen a tree fairy before.
His knees began to shake. His hands began
to shake. His axe fell to the ground with a thump.

"That is my tree! Please don't cut it down!" cried the tree fairy. The wood-cutter was so frightened he could not say a word.

"Please don't cut down my tree," begged the tree fairy. Her eyes were full of tears.

The wood-cutter tried hard to speak.

"Well..." he began.

"Well..." he began again.

"Well, all right, I won't," he said at last.

"I won't cut your tree down if you don't want me to."

"Oh, thank you!" said the tree fairy.
"How kind you are! And now I will do something for you. I will give you three wishes. No matter what in the world you wish for, your next three wishes will come true." Then the tree fairy was gone.

The wood-cutter picked up his axe and ran all the way home.

He told his wife about the tree and the tree fairy.
"We can wish for a real house, with many windows,"
  said the wood-cutter.
"Or even a tall castle!" said his wife.

"We can wish for a cart, and a goat to pull it,"
  said the wood-cutter.
"Or even a shining carriage, with white horses!"
  said his wife.

"We can wish for fine new clothes," said the
wood-cutter.

"Or even strings of pearls and ruby rings!" said his wife.

"We can wish for anything we want!"

"We must think hard before we wish," said the
wood-cutter.

"Yes, we must be sure to make good wishes," said his wife.

They talked for a long time.
They thought of many wishes.

At last the wood-cutter grew hungry.
He was sorry he had left his bag of bread and bottle of tea in
the forest.
"Is supper ready yet?" he asked.
"Of course not," said the wood-cutter's wife.
"It is much too early for supper."

"Will it be ready soon?" asked the wood-cutter.
"Supper will be ready when it is time for supper,"
 said his wife.
"Yes, I know," said the wood-cutter. "But I am hungry now.
 I wish I had a nice piece of sausage right now."

Clatter-bump! Clatter-bang!
A loud noise came from the chimney. And down fell a
great long piece of sausage onto the floor.

"Oh, what a fool you are!" shouted the wood-cutter's wife. "You have wasted a wish!"

"Oh dear," said the wood-cutter. "So I have."

"You could have wished for a whole pig!" said the wood-cutter's wife. "You could have wished for a whole farm, with a hundred pigs! Only a fool would wish for just one sausage!"

"You are right. You are right. I am sorry," said the wood-cutter.

"You could have wished for a golden crown! You could have wished for a whole barrel of gold! And you wished for a sausage!"

"I know," the wood-cutter said.

"I am really very sorry," the wood-cutter said.

The wood-cutter's wife scolded and scolded.
Soon the wood-cutter put his hands over his ears.
"Please stop!" he said.

But the wood-cutter's wife would not stop.
"A sausage! A sausage! A sausage!"
she shouted, over and over again.

At last the poor wood-cutter could stand no more.
"Stop! Stop! Stop!" he cried.
"I don't want to hear any more about the sausage!
I wish that the sausage were stuck to the end of
your nose!"

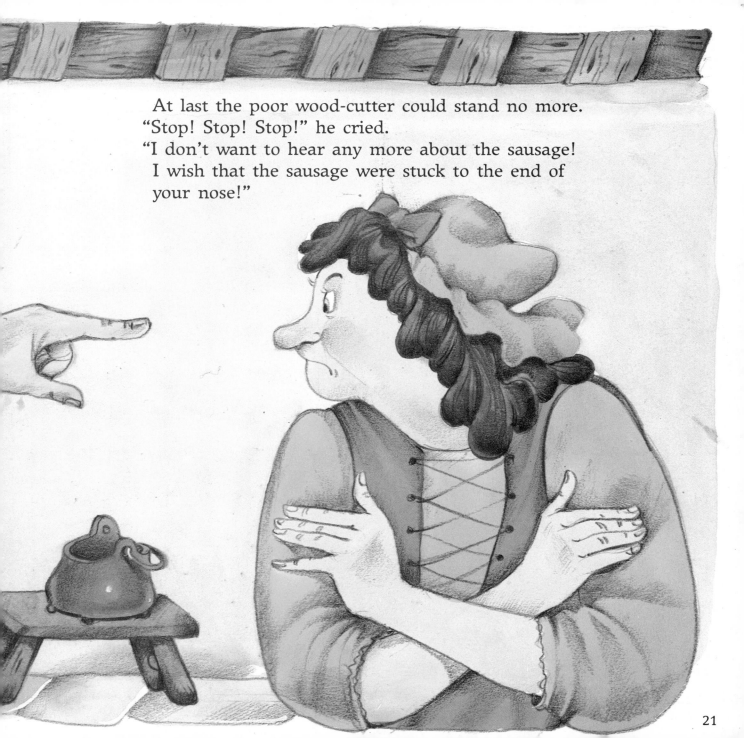

And it was.
The great long piece of sausage was stuck to the end of the wood-cutter's wife's nose.

The wood-cutter's wife pulled on the sausage.
It did not come off.
The wood-cutter pulled on the sausage.
It stayed where it was.
The wood-cutter and his wife pulled together.
They pulled until they were tired.

Pulling did no good at all. The great long piece of
sausage was still stuck to the end of the wood-cutter's
wife's nose.

"Do something!" said the wood-cutter's wife.
"You have one wish left!"

The wood-cutter looked hard at his wife's nose.
"It is not so very bad," he said. "I could get used to it,"
he said. "If we had a whole barrel of gold, I think I
could get used to it," he said.

"But I am sure that I could not!" cried the wood-cutter's wife. And so the wood-cutter had to use his last wish. "I wish that the sausage would come off the end of your nose," the wood-cutter said.

Plop!
The great long piece of sausage fell from the end of the
wood-cutter's wife's nose.

It landed in a white dish that was on the table.
The wood-cutter looked at the sausage.
The wood-cutter's wife looked at the sausage.

"It's time for supper now," she said.
"We might as well eat the sausage right away."

And that is what they did.